Nine Strange and Curious Tales

of Criminals, Fools, and the Macabre

JEREMY BECK

First Print Edition, 2020

ISBN: 978-1-7330432-9-8

To the memory of Fredric Brown, whose Nightmares and Geezenstacks both inspire and unnerve

CONTENTS

ON THE BEACH

JUDITH CROSSED the weather-worn bridge, over a narrow glistening inlet, to the empty beach. The late burst of summer heat was too compelling to ignore and since tourist season was now only a complicated memory, she had felt duty-bound to turn off the computer and finish her studies for the day. Now on the other side, away from the dirt and gravel lane she had followed to reach the bridge, Judith paused to remove her sandals and loosen her pulled-back hair.

Although the sand beneath her feet remained warm from the day's caress of the sun, the wind had come up and now began to whip along the coast. Walking at first, and perhaps encouraged by the wind, her steps unconsciously and gracefully became her own improvised dance. Alone on the beach, she felt unusually free, and her mad twirling kicked up puffs of sand all around her while her figure splashed long shadows against the bridge receding behind.

Worn out from her joyous spinning, Judith collapsed on the beach, letting the sand freely sift through her tangled hair. She gazed through her dizziness at the early dusk and

1

watched the stars slip beyond their daylight curtain, teasing out a sliver of the moon.

Her mind without warning swept her back to the heart of the summer and a love that had ended too quickly. She tried to forestall the sadness that accompanied the memory, but the melancholy sensation of laying on the sand in the dying light of the day washed over her before she could mount a defense. It was then that Judith felt something sharp, though not uncomfortably so, inch its way across her outstretched right palm. She flicked her wrist, but the feeling didn't change. She sat up and looked at her hand, expecting to discover some sort of tiny annoying insect perhaps, but she found nothing of consequence.

She gazed at the ocean, the lapping waves, shaking her hand, trying to dispel the growing soreness. The discomfort seemed to lessen, and Judith's thoughts trailed back to that last afternoon. It was only a silly game of croquet, and why did he care what the neighbors thought anyway? They weren't friends of hers, not really, only acquaintances that she saw every so often at the beach. It was important to be civil to one's neighbors, she thought, to engage in conversation, share a potluck now and then, a friendly game of cards. Someone had pulled out an old croquet set; all right, playing croquet was pretentious, maybe, but we can try it out, no big deal. But he had played poorly and there was some rude comment, and no, they're not my friends, and then after an uncomfortable night of unremembered disturbing dreams, he'd left, just like that.

Judith shook her hand again, as the aching returned, more forcefully now. She recalled that at first she couldn't understand why a boorish remark during a summer game of croquet would cause the breakup of a newish relationship, until she admitted to herself that it wasn't the cause, but an excuse, and that he probably had been looking for any pretext to leave. At least they hadn't been seeing each other long enough for his leaving to break her heart, she thought. It's just that his departure, the context of it, seemed so ridiculous to her, that it offered no real chance of closure.

Her review of this history was interrupted yet again by the insistent throbbing in her hand. It was too soon for her to panic, even as the aching steadily grew in intensity. She wondered if, perhaps, she had developed a cramp in her palm, that she had been working too hard that afternoon, typing too long at the computer, that she had developed some sort of tendonitis. There was that time during her junior year, when she had been on a hard deadline to get a research paper finished, when she had typed for nearly six hours straight, and the next morning her wrists were pounding, screaming at the abuse. She had vowed to take better care of herself after that painful experience, and hadn't she? Didn't she take regular breaks now, get up, stretch, walk around, heat up the kettle or freshen a drink?

She began rubbing her hand deliberately, firmly. She was confused, for this vexing feeling in her hand, a feeling that now caused her real pain, reminded her not at all of the tendonitis she had previously suffered, to the extent that she could recall it. Her massaging became more vigorous, she was now pressing deep into her palm, trying to ease the relentless sense of unusual pressure, now reaching a higher level of intensity she was sure she had never experienced before.

Her hand stinging now in a torture of continuous, deep

pulsing, Judith slapped the beach with her ringing fingers in the hope that somehow the increasing pressure, a pressure that had transformed into a bizarre twisting sensation, would finally stop.

It did not.

The waning crescent moon and its drape of stars mirrored Judith's contorted horror as her hand, in a final cascade of agony, ripped itself from her body and disappeared into the array of black and diamonds that floated above her.

**

THREAD

A FUNNY little something – a thread?

He noticed it in passing, brushed at it, without a second thought. He adjusted his new dress shirt, wondering if the color was OK – a light, peaceful shade of green. Then he added what he considered a nice tie, one of his favorites, which made him feel comfortable and confident, perhaps for no rational reason, but the effect was real, so – there you go.

The day that unfolded for him brought nothing unusual, not even a flicker of a memory that anything especially had caught his attention that morning.

So at the end of his day, on this particular day, he carefully removed the tie he admired, the one with such power, almost like a totem, and hung it on the rack, next to the more common choices. Undoing his shirt then, becoming ever more calm with each button unjoined, he noticed it again or saw another little something – funny.

A thread? On his lower abdomen, just to the right (from his perspective) of his belly button or navel – "belly button" was such a childish phrase, a holdover from the shadows of his toddler days. Now fifty, it seemed absurd to utter – "Doctor, what is this, next to my belly button?"

It wasn't a hair and didn't seem to be a loose – what? A thread?

He brushed at it again, more deliberately, with attention. Nope – not budging. It was short, odd, a kind of off-brown color, not black, not maroon, but in that ballpark, a darkish hue. Just long enough to grip the end between the thumb and forefinger, but to actually pull on it brought pain, just a twinge, but still, quite definite.

He pulled again – "what the - ?" – with the same resulting sharpness, a pain a little more determined, so he stopped, and thought, "to hell with this," and went back to the end of his day, as it had been, as usual, as expected, except for this – what? – a thread?

Undressed now, he tried to ignore this bothersome detail. Such an intrusion – no, it wouldn't ruin his evening. After carefully hanging up his shirt and pants, he stowed his socks and underwear into the hamper. He then turned on the shower, carefully adjusting the temperature, finding just the right balance, for him, of hot and cold. "Sort of a *mezzo-forte*," he mumbled to himself.

The water rushing down his back soothed him; the steady rhythm and heat providing a sense of comfort. He knew he shouldn't be bothered by this thread, that giving it such a presence in his thoughts served to only agitate him further. He fingered it again – "what is this blasted thing, damn it?"

He considered calling the "Ask-a-Nurse" service offered by his health insurance plan through work. He had used that service once before, when he had had a blazing sore throat and was running a constant temperature of 101 degrees. The nurse to whom he had spoken had been very helpful. In fact, and in spite of his feeling so ill, he had enjoyed their conversation. She had been an intelligent thoughtful woman, considerate of his condition, and seemed to sincerely want to help him. He wondered if she might answer should he decide to call.

But a sore throat and a temperature, that was one thing. It was explainable, perhaps unremarkable. But this? What? "I have a thread, or something, string-like, protruding from my abdomen. It's short, darkish in color. Not a stitch, no – I've not had an operation, not recently, anyway. It hurts when I pull at it, to try to dislodge it. I don't know how long it's been there – I just noticed it today, undressing at home, after work."

He turned off the water. No, he couldn't say that – it was ridiculous. It would make him sound … disturbed, even. This is what he thought, how it would sound to him, if he were answering the call.

Drying himself off, he realized he had been so absorbed in his problem, he had forgotten to actually wash; the soap lay dry in the rack. He cursed, debating whether to get back into the shower and wash, or wait until morning. "Well, I'm already dry, so forget it."

His robe on now, he made his way to the kitchen. "A light snack," he considered to himself, "will calm my nerves." It was the middle of summer, and the heat and humidity led to his diminished appetite. He assembled a kind of fruit salad, cutting up apples, pears, bananas, and adding some blueberries and grated parmesan cheese on top. He enjoyed the mixture of bright flavors and savored the interplay of textures and sounds, the hard crunch of the apple next to a sensual slide into a banana slice. He made a mental note to re-stock his supply.

Having finished and feeling relaxed, his mind wandered back to the thread. He pulled open his robe and there it was, still present, still annoying. He teased it again with his fingers, but the area around its base, where it emerged from his skin, was now a little red from when he had pulled on it before, and his touching the thing irritated it further.

Or so he thought.

Was it a play of the fading sunlight, as the sun gradually disappeared below the horizon? Or just the result of some cross-ventilation from the air conditioner working against the heat of the day? No. The thread had moved. Back and forth and around. Curling and uncurling. Independent movement. Having nothing to do with his touch or the present environment.

Like an antenna. Or a tail.

His teeth started chattering and his heartrate spiked. Then he blacked out.

*   *   *

The recovery of consciousness was a slow fade, an inversion of the summer night that now descended. The kitchen light was on, and it pierced his eyes as he blinked looking up, sprawled out on the linoleum floor. He weakly touched his temple, now bruised and tender from where he had hit the ground. There was no blood, and he briefly felt lucky until his memory returned and he shot a look at his stomach, wincing as he leaned up.

The thread was gone, and there was a pinhole of blood in its place. Along the floor he spotted a small trail of blood, really just an intermittent squiggle, that ended at the edge of an air-conditioning vent. He swallowed hard, trying to comprehend the truth that confronted him, that something… some*thing*? … had worked its way… *out* of him.

Pulling himself up and staggering over to the kitchen sink to get a drink of water, he leaned on the counter. And as a headache slowly began to pound into his reality, he caught himself wondering:

"Was that the only one?"

***

HERE'S WHAT I BEEN TOLD ABOUT IT

IT ALL STARTED early one mornin' on Interstate 65 south of the Hardin County line. Don't know if it was road rage, or the driver of the red Chevy was high, or the moon was still beamin' down the crazies, but it sure turned into some nasty bizness. Here's what I been told about it:

The weather was fine – no rain and the pavement dry. It was dawn, but visibility good. The driver of a semi was just headin' south, on his usual route, nothin' different. So the deal is, he tried to pass a red Chevy. Well, the driver of the red Chevy – that's Conners, you know him? – well, he fired a pistol at the semi, shattering the glass of the cab door. Fortunately, the shot missed and didn't hit the driver 'cuz he discreetly dropped back. He took the license number of the Chevy and called it into the police.

The driver of the semi, well, he supposed that was the end of it and just thought hisself lucky that all he caught was some bits of glass. But then he pulls off just shy of Tennessee and spots the Chevy at a gas station right there at the exit, with Conners filling up. So he calls the police again and, since they already have his name and such, figures he's done what's needed and takes off.

You'd've done the same.

The police now, two of 'em, quick as anything, swoop in to pick Conners up. Turns out there's also two women in the car, just sittin'. The police tell Conners he's under arrest, order the women out of the car, and help Conners push the Chevy away from the gas pumps. (Don't ask me why they don't cuff him right away, I don't know – it's easy enough to quarterback these things). Conners, if you can believe it, and calm as anything, then says he wants to get a cup of coffee – what? – but the one cop says, "Hell, no," and promptly handcuffs him. At this juncture, the other officer sees a shoe protruding from under a quilt on the back seat of the Chevy and, expecting to find the body of a shooting victim, he pulls off the cover and finds himself facing two pointed pistols in the hands of Kylie Dixon and hears a sulfurous threat to kill him. (Yes, *that* Kylie Dixon – I don't know who them two gals was).

Anyhoo, the officer who cuffed Connors, well he's distracted by the commotion and gets slugged on the back of the head by Conners while his partner, who's been starin' at the barrels, is severely pistol-whipped by Kylie Dixon, breaking the partner's jaw, knocking out his teeth and beatin' him into unconsciousness. The partner put up a good fight back and got in some hard licks, but Kylie Dixon just had the element of surprise always in his favor. The operator of a gas station across the way sees the beating from his office window, orders his son to call the police, grabs his rifle, and fires at the departing Chevy as it squeals off into the countryside.

Oh, the officers are all right. That one got knocked around pretty bad, but he's gettin' fixed up, so I been told.

But here's the rest of it. Later, turns out, them thugs abandon the Chevy, and the four of 'em (the thugs and the girls) tromp through the woods over to the farm of a Mr. Edgar Barstow in Monroe County where Conners approaches the Missus, draws his pistol, and orders her to get them some clothes. He then takes her to the barn to bandage up a big cut on the head of Kylie Dixon. (I told you the officer got in some good licks hisself). After this ministration, Kylie Dixon cuts the Barstow's outside phone line, Conners commandeers one of the family's cars, orders Barstow and his daughter into the car at gunpoint, and drives off. Yeah, their hearts was beatin' hard and you know they was prayin' to the Lord.

And them prayers worked, 'cuz the good news is, no member of the Barstow family was physically harmed, but you can bet they was kept in fear by the flourished weapons and threats. The father and daughter and the car was finally released in McCreary County. Conners apparently offered the daughter ten dollars for the clothes, which she rightly refused. Conners, Kylie Dixon, and the two women (I never did find out who they was) were hunted down and found about 5 P.M., sleepin' in a barn on the Tooley farm near the McCreary and Wayne County line, just a mile or so from where they'd left the hostages and the car. Conners lay sleeping with his pistol in ready reach, and the slumbering Kylie Dixon had his pistols in equal readiness.

They was convicted of armed robbery, malicious striking and wounding with intent to kill, and for carrying concealed deadly weapons. Crazy stuff.

Them girls? Told ya – don't know. Don't know what happened to the driver of the semi neither. Guess he got his window fixed all right. Hell, I prolly woulda turned 'round and headed north after sumpin' like that. Oh, it ain't hard to turn one-a them semis 'round – just gotta get off at an exit and cross the overpass if you don't have room otherwise. Anyway, figure they got a buncha time – who knows. Gimme another – that's all I been told about it.

**

CREEPY CRAWLEY

IT WAS ONE of those summer evenings where the sunset is flush with thoughts of rain. A downpour was certain, but all was still, quiet; thunder had yet to intrude upon my young son's peaceful sleep. My wife was out having a rare drink with friends and I had just finished singing a few children's songs while tucking our boy in for the night. Now I had settled myself downstairs with a favorite glass of wine and a good book.

Recently I had thought to go back to reading a beloved author from my youth. I had grown weary of modern irony and gratuitous violence fluffed up as "meaningful commentary" and so I skimmed the available titles on my bookshelf, seeking relief. After some private debate, it was finally Jack London who called to me and I pulled out a dusty paperback copy of some of his short stories.

As the wind outside began to pick up, I had just started to read "A Thousand Deaths" when I thought I heard my son sing a kind of tune, softly. But this wisp or fragment of melody lasted for such a brief instant, that I posited it likely had been only my imagination. For when the weather is wild in the dark of night, even a familiar place may feel less like a sanctuary and more as an unstable refuge. Add to that a tale of a mad scientist coupled with a fine chardonnay and, well, playful imagination becomes a plausible result.

I shook my head to clear it and thought to return to London, when the rain that had threatened began to cast itself to the earth, so I stopped my musing to get the open windows in the kitchen shut. Then, I heard him again, and knew I was not imagining his song:

"Creepy crawley, creepy crawley
Up your face and into your eyes
Where it kills you with a bite."

I was not overly shocked to hear this ditty; apparently he had heard some child sing a variation of it on the playground a day or two before and he had already sung it to me and my wife. Then, as now, he sang this verse in a light-hearted manner, and when we had heard him sing it to us before, we had smiled and only gently voiced our disapproval of this lyric, thinking of it as a cousin to a Grimm's fairy tale, meant to provide a shudder and perhaps some lesson, but nothing more. Mainly I was perturbed that he was no longer asleep or had yet to go to sleep. I went back up the stairs and peeked into his room. There were dim shadows thrown from his night-light. These in combination with the now insistent lightning flashes which shown through the closed curtains in his room accompanied by aggressive thunderclaps created a greater sense of unease within me than would reasonably be the case. But when I looked in his bed I saw nothing unusual;

my son was sleeping soundly, without showing a care in the world.

Sure now that I had heard the little rhyme, I attributed it to his own lively imagination, which I thought probably continued to be active even in rest. After all, he was forever fighting dragons or pirates and such, lashing out with a cardboard sword and dagger we had made together a few weekends past. Would it be so out-of-the-ordinary for his imaginings to continue in dreams?

I continued down the stairs, back to my chardonnay (refreshing the glass) and Jack London's tales. I must have dozed off, because I awoke sharply, feeling that something had been on my cheek. I brushed it away, whatever it had been, and then looked around to see what had disturbed me, but saw nothing. The rain was continuing to fall, and I wondered about the cellar, hoping water had not leaked in. We lived in an old, but beautifully restored Victorian home, with exquisite woodwork. My wife and I had been deeply attracted by this lost craftsmanship when we had decided to buy the home, but had not fully considered the issues attached to its needed upkeep. The cellar itself presented a variety of challenges. Paved with brick set into a packed dirt floor, during heavy rains the water often seeped through the home's rock foundation and gathered in unwelcome pools. It would have been terribly expensive to fully correct the problem, so my wife and I had simply resolved to address the leakage as this occurred, to try and prevent major damage to the items we had stored below.

There was an easy entrance into the cellar, from a back staircase just behind the pantry next to the kitchen. I was through that door and half-way down when I thought I heard again my son's lilting voice:

"Creepy crawley, creepy crawley
Up your face and into your nose
Where it kills you with a bite."

I was irritated by this second singing incident but as I was already entering the cellar and could see that, yes, water was leaking in, I put off reinvestigating the situation with my son. My wife and I had already moved certain boxes of stored books and family photographs onto shelves we had installed, but there were still some tools lying about from various spring gardening projects. I gathered these up out of harm's way and piled them onto an empty shelf when there was a loud crack of thunder and all the lights went out.

It was just as I was fumbling my way towards where I knew the stairs should be that I felt a kind of odd itching sensation in my left nostril. At first I thought it was merely an allergic reaction to the ever-present dust and mold that thrived in the cellar. As I wiggled my nose to try and tame the bothersome feeling I sneezed and suddenly there was a very sharp pinch, as if a small pin had been pushed towards the inside of my nostril. Admittedly, my response was perhaps unnaturally panicked as I pawed at my nose while simultaneously blowing out of the left nostril. Still, in spite of this unwanted distraction, I did reach the stairs and the unpleasantness stopped as soon as I climbed out of the cellar.

There was the blackout to contend with so I forgot about my nose (which no longer bothered me at all, suggesting that, indeed, I had experienced some sort of allergic reaction while down in the cellar) and I also forgot about my son's singing, as I looked for the flashlight we always kept in one of the kitchen cupboards. Of course, just as I found the thing buried under layers of hand towels, extra batteries, and other odds 'n ends, the lights shuddered back on.

From these tedious exertions, the dulling effect of the wine had dissipated and I was no longer interested in London's tales of mystery, adventure, and surprise. The clock on the mantle indicated my wife should be home within the hour, so I thought to empty the dishwasher in advance of her arrival when – yet again – I heard the tranquil, melodious sound of my son's sweet voice:

> "Creepy crawley, creepy crawley
> Up your face and into your ear
> Where it kills you with a bite."

Well, that third repetition was too much for me to tolerate. Was he merely pretending to be asleep, teasing me, forcing me to climb the stairs to his room, where he would appear angelic and unknowing, by his silent and steady breathing declaiming innocence of any knowledge of these verses he spun these late hours after his bedtime?

With some annoyance I took to the stairs, determined to make sure the boy was actually asleep. And so if he was, then what? Wake him to tell him not to sing while sleeping? That hardly seemed fair, akin to my wife blaming me for snoring, when one had no control over such things while unconscious. She would try to make me feel guilty for disturbing her rest by what she claimed were certain eruptions worthy of an elephant, but as I pointed out to her, Where was her proof? There were no recordings, I had only her word for the claim.

I had now gained the top of the staircase, and with my hand steady on the bannister, I noted yet again the beauty of the carving on the newel, how the flowers intertwined and in shadow appeared to become fully three-dimensional, inviting me to breathe in their perfume, which almost seemed impossibly real in that midnight hour. It is not clear to me what happened next, for as I leaned in closer to the ornamentation, I felt a sharp twinge on my right cheek, as if while shaving the razor had slipped, and it so caught me off guard, that when my hand flew to the spot in reaction, leaving the bannister, something, too, entered my right ear, and the gushing pain was a surprise, both in its arrival and its intensity, as if a kind of gnawing was present and growing.

*   *   *

Later, when I awoke in the hospital, learning that my wife – having arrived home just in that heightened moment of my agony – had called 911, not having any idea why I was screaming, I was surprised to find my right ear completely bandaged up. Or I assumed it was bandaged up, but in fact, you see, as I later discovered, my ear was completely gone. None of the doctors could proffer a reasonable explanation as to how this had happened, how it was that only slivers of skin and a slight hole in the side of my head was what remained when I was brought into the emergency room. I was assured, however, that there were options for reconstructive surgery, which I did later pursue.

I am pleased to report that those options were successful, at least from the extent of outside appearances. It is only upon a close examination that one can detect any anomaly on the right side of my head. But I was less fortunate with my hearing, for however it was that my right ear went missing, aural perception went with it. And so you may understand, my growing nervousness on certain evenings, when my left ear discerns, or think it detects, a certain whimsical-sounding fragment of melody, floating down from an upstairs bedroom.

***

CHESTER'S TIRES

THIS STORY is of the kind that begins with some headshaking, in a this-is-hard-to-believe sort of way. The circumstances then appear to turn out badly for those involved, before a creative solution emerges at the close.

Take it from me, that these circumstances and the details of what I'm about to share with you are not significantly disputed. While I admit to a lack of personal knowledge, the unnamed party who told me this story lived in Adams County about the time these events took place and is a credible person with the highest integrity. After working with him or in association with him in one capacity or another for over three and a half decades, I think you can take my word on that.

Well, now - the story, and I'll retell it as best as I can.

For several years prior to 1972, Chester Grant accumulated and stored some used vehicle tires on a farm he owned in that same said Adams County. He had gathered up mostly automobile and truck tires, but a curious trespasser might also have viewed a scattering of tractor tires, kids' wagon tires, mower tires, bicycle tires, and even a pair of wheelchair tires. By 1972, Chester's farm was home to somewhere in excess of a hundred such tires and it was Chester's intention to sell them to the Chinese government for their petroleum content. How and when Chester had acquired this notion is one of the unfortunate unknowns in this account, as it would likely have provided further interest in the tale, but since indeed the background to Chester's scheme is lost to history, it would be foolish to spend any time fretting over the matter.

In any event, when the sale to the Chinese did not reach fruition, Chester encountered financial difficulty, fell into debt, and sought assistance from his friend, Junior Stevens. To bring Chester's indebtedness current, Junior agreed to borrow $75,000 and become a partner in the anticipated sale of the tires. As Junior's particular assets were insufficient collateral for a $75,000 loan, Chester conveyed the tire storage property to Junior who then obtained the loan by encumbering the property as well as his personal dwelling.

At this point I should emphasize what I earlier had indicated, i.e., that the source of this story is an old acquaintance (well, perhaps a friend), and observe that I have met neither of the gentlemen who are the principals in this story. As far as I can tell from their participation in these events, they may have been swept up in their fantasies of wealth to the extent that reality became a distant horizon. How Chester and Junior even planned to make contact with the Chinese to effect their sale of the tires, well, even that aspect of the plan is ripe for speculation. It could be the case that neither one of them had thought through the transaction that far. And certainly it may be said our boys hadn't yet learned that the seduction of easy riches often leads to infertile pastures.

Well, with the intended sale still not consummated, Junior Stevens, too, fell on hard times and became delinquent in payment of the mortgage loan. In an effort to generate some income from the property, Junior sought an additional loan from the bank to improve a building on the premises for rental as an apartment. In preparation for an inspection from a bank officer, Junior undertook to have the property around the building cleaned up and this required relocation of some of the tires.

It is unclear if Chester raised objections to Junior's plans or if he calmly acquiesced. Whatever occurred, the relocation plan did not foresee certain contingencies. To perform the cleanup, Junior Stevens hired Tyler Watson and instructed him to roll the tires from around the building down a hill towards a great oak tree at the bottom. However, as Watson was rolling the tires as instructed by Junior, a neighbor, Ms. Sarah E. Haverman was unfortunately struck by said tires and suffered personal injury.

Ms. Haverman then hired a bright young attorney who, of course, sued everyone she could think of, ultimately winning the case. Trying to collect on the jury award was a challenge, however, because the main thing of value Chester and Junior had (forget about Tyler – he had nothing) was the property with all those accumulated tires lounging about. Ms. Haverman had no interest in conferring with the Chinese about anything, so, while she took the property, her attorney demanded that Chester and Junior convey the property to Ms. Haverman "tire-free."

The problem, of course, was going to be the process of removal, for the previous effort at relocating the tires had resulted in Ms. Haverman's unfortunate accident, and both Ms. Haverman's attorney and the judge overseeing the case (Judge Bernard Ravenscott, well-known in the region for his winning fried pork gravy) made clear to Chester and to Junior Stevens they were to do nothing that would potentially expose Ms. Haverman to any liability.

And they had ten days to do it.

On the first day, a Saturday, our boys drove out in a borrowed pick-up to Chester's farm (well, Ms. Haverman's farm). The accident and the lawsuit that followed had taken the matter into the heat of July. Chester and Junior (representing themselves, they had no money) had begged Judge Ravenscott to let them address the tire problem in the fall, after things had cooled off some. But Ms. Haverman's attorney objected, and the judge overruled the unhappy pair. The thing was, the two gentlemen knew the tires would no longer just be tires – at least some of them now harbored snakes and wasp nests and Lord knows what other unpleasantness (which is why Junior hired Tyler in the first place). So as they pulled up off the dirt road and parked near the accumulated mess, they both sighed and cursed, slamming the truck's doors as they set off on what they knew would be a bad day, probably a very bad day.

Chester had a foot up on a worn Firestone, as he and Junior surveyed the task before them. They had ten days, and while neither of them was especially mathematically-inclined, they had figured out the basic concept that if they filled up the truck's bed with as many tires as possible, and took as many loads as possible each day, the job should get done in time. Soon enough they got to it, always careful to look inside each tire before grabbing it, making sure there was nothing in there that would bite, sting, or otherwise cause personal vexation.

They hadn't yet solved what they were going to do with all these tires, but that didn't stop them from heading out with the first load. Let me remind you, fair reader, it was July, and not a pretty July either, with the heat coming off the state highway asphalt and those two driving a forlorn, unair-conditioned truck, accompanied by all the rattles and wheezing you might imagine it had (of which it had plenty). It was as they were getting closer to town that they figured after making it out with a first load, they deserved a treat.

Pulling into the drive-up Dairy Kone a mile or so out from the farm and about the same from town further on down the road, the discussion moved from tires to dip cones, which raised their spirits. They ordered from the lone kid behind the screen, a high schooler who was more interested in picking at his stubble of a beard than in doing anything else in the July heat. And as they leaned on the outdoor counter, licking the ice cream that was swiftly melting down the cones and onto their fingers, it was only then, glancing back at the truck, and beyond, that they saw something that made them both suddenly feel the harsh plunge of despair. For they'd left tires bouncing down that state highway like round rubber breadcrumbs, leading all the way they guessed back to the pile that remained at the farm.

Yes, they argued back and forth about who should've tied down what and the kind of knots that would've worked better and damn it now we gotta go pick up all them tires and it's like we've made no progress at all. The high school kid working the Dairy Kone just scratched at his stubble of a beard and said nothing.

Even with summer's long daylight hours, it was dark by the time they'd collected the last of the spilled tires, which in the process of picking them up had brought them back to where they'd started earlier that day. They cut more rope and tied the tires down in ways that gave them both a greater sense of security, that they wouldn't be going anywhere, but then they had to consider yet again what they were going to do with them, which they never had figured out, even when they had first started out with the initial load that day, supposing they'd work it out along the way.

The obvious place to go was the county dump, but they pretty much knew they'd only be let in with maybe one load. Chester never did hook up with the Chinese, so the notion of selling them like the plan that had started it all, that idea lasted for only a whisp of a minute. They went ahead to the dump anyway, figuring they might as well get rid of their one load and then try to resolve what to do with the rest of the tires after that.

They drove slower this time, keeping the rattles sounding more like a series of low moans instead of some continuous prattle. The night was cooler, so that helped their mood. But because it was late, the dump was closed, the chain-link fence padlocked shut. Briefly, they thought about just tossing everything over the fence, but they knew the sheriff would be right after them for doing it, since the whole county knew about the tire fiasco and the court judgment against them.

But where to go…?

Chester and Junior sat in the truck, motor off, smoking cigarettes. Junior was drumming his fingers, still sticky from the ice cream, on his right knee.

What do we do with 'em...?

It's been said that "necessity is the mother of invention." And maybe the day's many dramatic and frustrating turns brought a somewhat higher power to the boys' stunted imaginations. Well, perhaps all that didn't make any difference to Junior, but here's the thing: Chester got an idea.

It was an unusual thought, and especially so for Chester. On the other hand, he'd been tinkering with the notion of doing business with the Chinese, so it all could be considered of one piece. He asked Junior, "How much coils of rope we got in back?" Junior shrugged, so he got out to look. "A lot."

Chester cranked the engine back up. He had a plan which he explained to Junior along the way, who just shrugged in response.

They drove out to Otter's Creek Park and pulled into the parking lot by the playground. It was near pitch-black out, but they could see good enough by the headlights. Chester took a length of rope, sort of rough measured it out by hand, cut it, and swung it up over a sturdy lower branch of a nearby oak tree. Junior brought over a good automobile tire from out of the truck bed, and they tied it to the rope.

It would be just the first of the many tire swings they'd rig up that night. And they were just getting started.

By the end of the week, Chester and Junior had slung probably a hundred or so tire swings, scattered in probably every park in Adams County. And after they had done probably ten or so in the final park, they set up a few more in random spots in the surrounding undeveloped woods. Since they used to run around in those woods as kids, they thought probably the youngins still did, and wouldn't it be fun for them to find an unexpected and unexplained tire swing in the middle of nowhere?

The boys' tire-swing spree – always carried out in the middle of the night 'cause they knew they might get in trouble for it – found them at the end of that week with only a small inventory of tires left on the farm, and those would be the odd ones out, that scattering of tractor tires, kids' wagon tires, mower tires, bicycle tires, and the pair of wheelchair tires. That particular gathering would be the boys' last load, and the one they successfully dropped off at the county dump during regular working hours.

All around the county, as each day of that week had passed, there had been talk about the growing supply of tire swings emerging unbidden around the town and its environs. But the kids were happy with 'em, and even though everyone knew the likely source, no one stepped up to object and Ms. Haverman was in any case pleased the land was cleared off. She even didn't mind that one such tire swing was hanging off the big oak at the bottom of the hill where they had originally landed after the rolling, and figured she might even go swing on it herself one of these days (after she healed up).

And the good news is, neither Chester nor Junior got bit or stung while hauling and slinging up those tires. In the end, they counted themselves lucky and besides, who doesn't enjoy a tire swing?

***

THE CABINET

ONE OF HIS TASKS was to move boxes of files to the law firm's storage closet on the top floor of the building. This meant borrowing a hand truck from maintenance, stacking four or five boxes on the hand truck, and then wheeling the load out to the elevator. At first it was a tad awkward for him, maneuvering the hand truck into the elevator with all of that weight, but after a few trips he found a rhythm to the process and this helped the transfer go more smoothly.

The law firm had been keeping the boxes in the regular file room, but this soon proved to be unmanageable. It was as if the firm had become a collective of hoarders, insistent upon keeping every antique and unnecessary document close at hand. The boxes were stacked nearly shoulder high. Upon entering the room, one's impression was that of encountering a type of suffocating maze or labyrinth. An entranceway between two stacks of boxes revealed a further random series of aisles that passed into the depths of the room, like some pioneer had carved pathways into this wilderness of old depositions, faded transcripts, ancient correspondence, and outdated pleadings.

But over the course of the morning and afternoon, by dint of hard work, he made good progress; now the walls of boxes were dismantled, appearing more as a ruin rather than a fortress. He decided to take up one more load, before calling it a day.

The storage closet, so-called, was really a type of storage space that shared a segment of the building's top floor. There were dozens of such "closets" up there, defined by wooden frames of two-by-fours and separated by chicken wire. He had been unloading the boxes into the firm's unit from front to back, neatly trying to design a series of new aisles for future access. As he wheeled this final load in and rolled it towards the back of the closet, he noticed something tall lodged at the back of the space. He stopped and looked at it, wondering why he hadn't noticed it before. Covered by some kind of dark tarp, it almost melded into the shadow of a neighboring closet's file cabinets.

He moved towards it, curious. The tarp was a deep olive green, slightly military in appearance. It was unmarked, but encrusted periodically with certain dim stains. In touching it, the covering felt rough and was difficult to grasp, but he pulled it down and away from what was under it. In doing so, dust and other particles briefly fluttered around him, but then he could see it: a magnificent cabinet.

Made of a dark wood, perhaps mahogany, it was adorned with highly detailed carvings. It seemed out of place, stuck up there in storage. The carvings were intricate, with flowers, ribbons, bows, baskets and wreaths running along the top and both sides as well as outlining the door. On the bottom there was carved scenery, with ram's-head curved legs ending in animal-paw feet.

He didn't know much about such things, but to his eye it looked old, and likely valuable. His aunt had some antique furniture like this, tables and chairs from the nineteenth century, handed down through distant relatives. He wondered how long this cabinet had lived up there and to whom it belonged. On closer inspection, he saw it had a few scrapes and was covered in dust. He supposed it could have been left up there for years by some forgotten predecessor. He fancied it could be considered an armoire, a wardrobe, but why it would be languishing there, behind chicken wire, file cabinets, and boxes stacked up to his shoulders, he couldn't imagine.

The cabinet's door handle was of brass, colored dull by time and lack of use. He tried the handle, and although its movement was stiff, he was able to open the door. A thick, moldy stink emerged from the cabinet's interior. He unconsciously wrinkled his nose, and saw there was only one thing inside.

Hanging in the closet was a gentlemen's suitcoat. For its age, it appeared to be in remarkably good condition. Besides a musty smell, it otherwise looked fairly clean, albeit a bit faded in color. He couldn't place the year, but from the unfamiliar style, he thought it might be over 50, maybe over 70 years old. The coat was of a darker shade of charcoal, not quite black, with round magenta buttons. On impulse, he took it out of the closet, thinking to try it on, when he felt a kind of weight to the coat that didn't match its size and appearance. Feeling around and reaching into the pockets, he pulled out a small pistol. It felt unusually warm in his hand, and then time abruptly vanished.

When his consciousness returned, although still foggy, he realized he hadn't taken the elevator back down to his office, for he found himself in the stairwell, outside the door to the sixth-floor lobby. How had he gotten there? Had he walked down twenty flights of stairs without any awareness of the act? His breathing was slow, burdened. He stared at the concrete walls, wondering why someone had chosen to paint them a kind of bright mustard yellow.

Still breathing hard, he now remembered the pistol in his hand. He glanced down, and it seemed to be fading from view then reappearing. He recalled stumbling into the foyer on the sixth floor, the receptionist asking if he was OK, then nothing. It was then that an infinite rain of black dots appeared, furiously clouding his vision, burning through his eyes like a raging sandstorm, and he felt himself pull the trigger. The pulling felt familiar and he chuckled at the reverberating sound in the stairwell as the bullet hit the wall. The mustard yellow seemed to vibrate and then he heard the sirens, far off at first, then converging somewhere closer below. He pulled again – *click*. He chewed on his lower lip, dropped the empty pistol – was it still there? – and re-entered the sixth-floor lobby.

Bodies and blood.

***

THE WRATH OF THE LIBRARIANS

THE DEFENDANTS were college buds in their early twenties who hatched a plan to steal rare books from the special collections library at the University and sell them at auction in New York City. Their earliest musings began in January, but the actual robbery did not occur until the following December.

During that intervening summer, after months of idle discussion, these four geniuses decided in earnest to carry out the robbery, which led to months of research (about rare books, auction houses, Swiss Bank accounts, etc.), brainstorming, and planning. As the preparations moved forward, each of the four took on separate responsibilities: Dave Sturgis created aliases (e.g., "Justin Frist") with fictional backgrounds, set up email accounts for those aliases, and contacted the library and various auction houses. Dan Perry created disguises, drew floor plans and maps, and created false documents. Joey Murdock and Skeeter Johnson staked out the library to determine staffing and security, planned the getaway (e.g., got a car, planned the route, etc.), and generally financed the operation (e.g., made hotel reservations in New York and purchased tasty snacks for the trip).

The gang determined that the best time for the robbery would be December, just before the University's fall term ended. They also decided to use Tanenbaum's auction house, one of New York City's finest, to sell the stolen books. The plan involved only certain rare and very valuable books.

So, in early December, while posing as one "Justin Frist," they sent an email to Tanenbaum's "private sales department," claiming to be "in possession of rare books … worth millions," and seeking a meeting towards the end of the month. A few days later, "Frist" sent another email, apparently in response to Tanenbaum's reply, this time stating:

> I have a first addition [sic] Origin of Species by Charles Darwin, manuscripts that date back to the 1500s, and a collection of John James Audubon's Qquadrupeds [sic] and Birds of America. I know that these books are worth a lot…

The email concluded with a renewed request for a late December meeting.

Meanwhile, Sturgis, again representing himself as "Justin Frist," an out-of-town businessman, telephoned Mrs. Terry Stevens, the Special Collections Librarian at the University Library, to request an appointment to view several of the library's rare books, including: *Origin of Species*, *Illuminated Manuscripts*, and the John James Audubon collection. Mrs. Stevens agreed and scheduled the appointment.

The next day, "Frist" (aka Sturgis and Perry) sent an email from the University computer lab to Mrs. Stevens, confirming the appointment and again specifying an interest in "the famous Audubon books, the first addition [sic] Darwin, and any of the Illuminated Manuscripts."

A week later, the robbery was finally at hand and after months of scheming, this was the plan: all four men would enter the library, take the books by force, and run for it. They arrived at the library dressed as "old men" — makeup, wigs, hats, and costumes, such as one would typically see worn in a play or some other type of theatrical performance — but aborted the plan at the last minute. The exact reason for aborting is unclear; they may have caught a glimpse of a flaw in the plan or simply panicked, though it was suggested at trial that another student, unaware of the impending robbery, recognized one of them and asked what they were doing in those ridiculous costumes. In fact, the costumes were sufficiently ridiculous that two library employees, including the Head Librarian, Doris Greene, noticed them, but merely assumed some sort of college prank or goof.

Later that same afternoon — after aborting and fleeing — "Frist" called Mrs. Stevens and apologized for missing the appointment, claiming to have been out of town for work. He asked to reschedule for the next morning. Mrs. Stevens reluctantly obliged, and agreed that he could bring a friend to view the books as well.

When Sturgis, posing as "Justin Frist," arrived for the appointment the next morning, Mrs. Stevens was surprised by two things: (1) he was much younger than she had expected, and (2) he was wearing an unseasonably heavy coat, gloves, and hat. After establishing that the elevator was working and there were no cameras in the library, "Frist" asked if he could have his friend join them. When Mrs. Stevens agreed, he made a call on his cell phone and within a few minutes a second man arrived (Dan Perry) — wearing a heavy coat, a bandage on his face, and eyeglasses — who introduced himself as "Larry." Both men signed in with illegible signatures.

Things went swiftly downhill from there. Once inside the Special Collections Library, the two men wrestled Mrs. Stevens to the ground, and began zapping her in the arm with a pen-type stun gun, which caused a tingling sensation and left a small bruise, but did not cause any significant pain or lasting harm. Mrs. Stevens screamed, though she knew that no one could hear her from that location in the library, but she did not panic.

She later testified that, while being subdued, she felt the tingling, heard an electric humming and popping noise, and feared that she was being zapped with a stun gun. She was particularly unnerved, however, when Sturgis — whom she did not know — called her by her first name, warning her: "Terry, if you just keep on struggling, it will only hurt more. Do you want it to hurt more?" Greatly frightened by this threat, her awareness of the stun gun, and the hair-raising intimacy of the robber having used her first name so casually, Mrs. Stevens submitted and the two men bound her hands and feet with plastic zip ties. They also removed her glasses and covered her eyes with a stocking cap.

Sturgis and Perry then began to collect the seven "objects of cultural heritage" — some comprising multiple volumes or pieces — that Mrs. Stevens had set out in anticipation of the appointment, and prepared to carry them from the library by way of an elevator to a first-floor emergency exit. These seven "objects," all of which were eventually recovered undamaged, were later appraised by Tanenbaum's, and have been described as follows:

1. *Hortus Sanitatis, Ortus Sanitatis translate de Laten en Francois.*
    Paris, circa 1500.
    Two volumes, with four full-page woodcuts and approximately 450 woodcut illustrations in the text.
    Estimated value: $450,000.

2. Pencil drawings, believed to have been commissioned for *The Birds of America, Second Octavo Edition.*
    New York and Philadelphia, circa 1855.
    Twenty of a 21-piece collection (one drawing was on display, and hence, not with the collection at the time of the robbery).
    Estimated value: $50,000.

3. *A Synopsis of the Birds of North America*, by John James Audubon. (New York, 1839).
    Eight volumes, mostly unopened.
    Autographed by John James Audubon himself, as a gift to a friend.
    Estimated value: $10,000.

4. *On the Origin of Species by Means of Natural Selection*, by Charles Darwin.
    London, 1859.

First edition; rebound.
Estimated value: $25,000.

5. *Illuminated Manuscript, Devotional Calendar.*
England, circa 1425.
Sixty leaves, one full-page miniature, and elaborate
initials and illuminations throughout.
Estimated value: $200,000.

6. *The Birds of North America from Original Drawings,*
by John James Audubon.
London, 1827-1838.
Four (4) volumes, elephant folio, 435 hand colored
engraved plates.
Estimated value: $4,800,000.

7. *The Viviparous Quadrupeds of North America,*
by John James Audubon and John Bachman.
New York, 1845-1848.
Three (3) volumes, with 150 hand colored
lithograph plates.
Estimated value: $225,000.

There is some dispute as to whether the robbers
intended to take only certain objects or as much as they could
carry, but, as evidenced by their planning, they had clearly
foreseen that the objects they coveted would be very large
and heavy. Consequently, they brought with them a (pink)
bed sheet, which they laid out on the floor, for carrying the
objects. Apparently, even with their planning, however, they
had underestimated the sizes and weights, and they were

forced to abandon two of the *Birds of North America* volumes, which were left in the Special Collections Library, atop the pink bed sheet. They also abandoned other volumes, later, while fleeing from the librarians.

To return to the story, Sturgis and Perry had, in a matter of minutes, collected these seven objects — except for the two *Birds of North America* volumes that they had abandoned on the pink bed sheet, and one of the three *Quadrupeds of North America* volumes, which had become stuck in its drawer — and were preparing to abscond with them. According to the (revised) plan, they would take the "employee-only" elevator down to the first floor and escape through an emergency exit, where Murdock was waiting in a van (which they dubbed the "GTAV," i.e., the "get to and away vehicle") to drive them home to stash the "loot." Johnson was standing watch across the street.

Apparently, Sturgis and Perry had some difficulty operating the elevator, however. The Head Librarian, Ms. Doris Greene was in the library's basement at the time and, prompted by the unexpected "ding" of the elevator's opening doors, she turned her attention to see who would be using the elevator. She was startled when the doors opened to reveal not employees, but Sturgis and Perry, in their heavy coats and gloves, holding some of the library's most prized and valuable possessions.

Realizing that something was amiss, Ms. Greene started for the elevator, but Sturgis and Perry quickly got the doors closed and the elevator moving again. Alarmed, Ms. Greene ran up the stairs to Special Collections in search of Mrs. Stevens. Meanwhile, Mrs. Stevens had realized that, due to the department's security measures, Sturgis and Perry could not re-enter the Special Collections Department from the elevator, and she had begun to free herself to call for help. She yelled to Doris Greene that they were being robbed, and Ms. Greene wheeled around to pursue the robbers.

She caught up to them in a stairwell where they were attempting to open the emergency exit and, surprised by her arrival and aggressive confrontation, they dropped several objects — specifically, the two remaining volumes of the *Birds of North America* four-volume set (they had left two volumes atop the pink bed sheet in the Special Collections Department) and the two volumes of the *Quadrupeds* three-volume set (one of the three volumes had been left behind, stuck in its drawer in the Special Collections Department). Sturgis and Perry fled through the emergency door carrying five objects (*Hortus Sanitatis*, the 20 pencil drawings, *Synopsis of the Birds of North America*, *Origin of Species*, and *Illuminated Manuscript*), with Ms. Greene and other librarians in hot pursuit. Sturgis and Perry scrambled into the waiting van and Murdock sped away, though not before Ms. Greene had scratched the van with a key in an attempt to mark it for later identification.

Once the robbers had escaped, the police were called, but before the police could document the crime scene, some librarians collected the discarded objects and returned them to their proper places.

Murdock, who had borrowed the van from an uncle or a cousin, let Sturgis and Perry out several blocks away, went to drop off the van, and returned to pick up Sturgis and Perry in a different car. The three of them went home and hid the stolen objects in the basement of their residence, in a semi-hidden room — the entrance to the room was disguised to conceal the fact that they had marijuana growing in there. They then gathered up evidence related to the robbery, including planning documents, the disguises, and the stun pen, and disposed it all in a nearby dumpster.

Johnson, who was enrolled at the University, stayed on campus to take an exam. Having told their parents that they were going on a ski trip over Christmas break, the four men left town a few days later. But they actually drove to New York City to keep their appointment at Tanenbaum's and have the objects appraised. Just before Christmas, Sturgis and Johnson, claiming to be "Mr. Hill" and "Mr. Martin" — representatives of "Justin Frist," who they described as "a very private individual who was interested in selling some rare books through Tanenbaum's private sales service" — met with Tanenbaum's representative Stacey Margolis. After reviewing the objects for approximately 15 minutes, Ms. Margolis agreed that Tanenbaum's could sell the objects for "Mr. Frist." Johnson gave Ms. Margolis his cell phone number so that she could contact him and the four men returned home with the objects.

Meanwhile, police were investigating the emails that "Justin Frist" had sent to Mrs. Stevens from the account "Fristjustin@----.com." Email account records immediately revealed the series of emails between "Frist" and Tanenbaum's, and through some further investigation, the police determined that the emails had been sent from a computer lab at the University. By early January, the police, in concert with the FBI, had contacted Tanenbaum's and spoken with Ms. Margolis, who gave them the cell phone number that Johnson had given her at the close of the December meeting.

By early February, the police had linked that number to an account held by Johnson's father and had determined that Johnson was the primary user of that particular number. Following these leads, the police put together photo lineups and positively identified Sturgis and Johnson. This led to search and arrest warrants.

Police executed the warrants a few days later, apprehended the four men, and recovered all five objects (*Hortus Sanitatis*, the 20 pencil drawings, *Synopsis of the Birds of North America*, *Origin of Species*, and *Illuminated Manuscript*) undamaged. Police also recovered three stun guns (though not the "stun pen" allegedly used in the robbery), notes pertaining to planning of the robbery, and clothes worn by the men to the robbery and the meeting at Tanenbaum's.

The objects were returned to the University, the four men went to prison, and the librarians were roundly praised for their defense of the recovered objects. One wag later quipped that the four men's bloodlines could be traced back to Darwin's *Origin*, but that claim remains unconfirmed.

***

FINGERS

SHE LIT THE FIRE and the ritual began.

There was powder to cast into the flames, a certain preparation she had spent many weeks curing and pounding. She used her free hand to toss it in, causing the flames to sparkle followed by a thickening smoke of twisted colors, feverish reds and nearly-black purples. Her fingers on her other hand, the fingers required for this effort, were properly stained and ready. As the smoke expanded in whirling clouds around her, she stretched the prepared fingers, the fingers of her left hand. She stretched them widely and also forward, as far as they could reach. Moving closer to the firelight, if one were watching, it would be revealed that she stretched only the first three fingers of her hand, as the place where the fourth should be had long been only a stub of hard flesh. She mumbled now, something like words, perhaps more like guttural sounds, something not quite human, something primitive and unworldly, suited to the ragged shadows surrounding her effort. Her eyes focused hard on the stretching, and the fingers were taut and stiff, like branches of an ancient, gnarled tree, a tree that shook, buffeted by some silent hard wind, and the veins on the back of her hand, popping out, showing tributaries of blood pumping beneath the discolored skin, and imperceptively, did her fingers grow? Was it only her physical stretching, cast in shadowed obscurity and the flickering light of the fire that shaped the hallucination, the misperception of growth? She breathed heavier now, the mumbling, the sounds from her throat, never ceasing, she succumbed to the trance and its power took over, and - My God! - her fingers did grow, becoming longer, tendrils that pushed deep into the shadows of the churning smoke.

*   *   *

They were hiking, Claire and Susanne, into the backwoods of the state park. They had set out after lunch on this cool autumn day. The leaves had mostly fallen, and the crunch beneath their feet felt welcoming as they made their way under low branches, moving off the marked trail, exploring the terrain. They had been walking for hours when they discovered a patch of late-blooming blueberry bushes and enjoyed a quick snack, the berries' juice both tart and sweet. The taste reminded Claire of her time at summer camp, going on similar hikes with her bunkmates. That's where she and Susanne had first met and become friends. And now they went to the same college and were enjoying a weekend away from their studies.

They hopped over a shallow stream of run-off and Claire saw it first. The fallen tree – was it a tree? – drew her attention. It was perhaps twenty feet away, in a small clearing. She hesitated, her head slightly turned in curiosity, and then she walked towards it. Susanne, behind her, followed along, not immediately seeing what had attracted Claire's attention.

There were three odd-looking branches, aiming towards the late afternoon sky, swaying slightly in the evening wind.

As they drew closer, Susanne, too, found what they had taken to be a fallen tree strangely fascinating in its unusual shape. And then they saw that what they had perceived as branches were not attached to any tree. It was as if they had come directly out of the ground or been stuck into the ground. Both of them observed the way they curled ever so slightly at the top. It made them feel nervous, without knowing why.

Claire barely muttered, "They look like fingers."

Susanne nodded, although Claire didn't see the acknowledgment. Instead, her eyes focused on what she had considered to be the shading of the tree bark, but now, closer, the colors – deep reds and near-purples – confused her. They stopped – the air around them grew quiet, the smell of the damp earth flashed a memory of their summer camp days – and then the branches awkwardly stretched and weirdly grew before their eyes, and Susanne screamed, as the three branches lashed out, clasping Claire in their grip and pulling her down into the mud, crashing hard, and she struggled, thrashing in terror within the firm grip of the branches, screaming for help, but Susanne was frozen, shocked, unbelieving, and the three branches, those weird fingers from a bizarre nightmare, pulled Claire into the earth, beneath the soil, and she was gone.

*   *   *

The fire was out and she slept now, her fingers still stained, but now also muddy. There was blood on her lips, the taste both tart and sweet.

***

I CLYMEE

HAVE YOU EVER had the feeling there was something behind you? You'd turn around, perhaps feeling silly and foolish, but still – there was some compulsion to look. And if you didn't turn around, if you didn't look, there'd be that continuing sense of something not being quite right, of something being…off?

When I was a kid, I could be ruled by such compulsive thoughts, feelings, and behavior. Remember this one? "If you step on a crack, you'll break your mother's back." Who on Earth made that one up? How many little kids (like me) believed it or didn't believe it, but didn't want to take the risk that there was even a spidgen of truth to it? As a result, I skipped and jumped over hundreds and perhaps thousands of sidewalk cracks in my life.

No, I don't worry about breaking my mother's back anymore.

And then there was the constant effort to avoid doing what I thought might result in my inverting myself. Let me explain: if I turned around a certain way – say, I turned to the left – in order to get back to where I had started, I had to turn back to the right. I could never in a zillion years allow myself to continue turning left, making a complete 360-degree circle to return to my starting point. If I ever did that, and sometimes I experimented and tried doing that, well, I felt just … wrong. Like I had twisted or inverted myself into some other shape or space. The change I felt in such moments was real, and the discomfort so strong, that at the first opportunity I would have to turn completely back around the opposite way to get back to my "real" position.

As I entered my teens, I gradually grew out of such obsessive behavior, and my thoughts did not continue to careen in such disturbing directions. And yet the sensation of something appearing behind me never seemed to fade away. Even in my twenties, I still would feel a sense of "something" being there, and would indulge the necessity of turning to look, only to see nothing.

I would chastise myself in those days, how I was acting immaturely, that such feelings and forebodings were childish, leftover anxiety from my younger years. I fought the need to turn and soon congratulated myself for overcoming this compulsion. After a while, I stopped having to fight the need to turn around and look behind me, and soon that vague sense of something not being quite right passed from my reality.

It was perhaps only a few months after this that something odd happened. I was returning home from an evening out with friends. We had gone to see a play, and then gathered afterwards for drinks. The bar was crowded with loud music and a constant chattering din. I felt overwhelmed by the noise which only made me feel even more tired than

I already was, so I didn't stay long. After a couple of drinks and a futile attempt to delay my departure, my friends chose to remain at the bar as I stepped out into the sultry August air. When the heat and humidity are up, the night air in Louisville is more Southern than not, thick and pressing.

My apartment was only a few blocks further from the bar where my friends were still gathered. As I've previously shared, I had reached that stage where I was no longer giving in to thoughts or concerns of something being behind me as I made my way home, enjoying the quiet of the night after the clamor of the bar. It was then, quite suddenly, I felt a shocking weight on my back and a strange high-pitched voice whispered in my left ear, "I Clymee."

I shook my body hard the instant this happened, twisting left and right, stunned by the occurrence. My heart was pounding; it was instantly a fight-or-flight moment, yet it was over almost as soon as it had happened.

Standing there, half-stooped, I caught my breath and looked quickly around me. There was no one and no immediate doorway in which to hide or alley to dash into. The streetlights were on and I could see nothing unusual. There was no passing traffic and I did not hear running feet or a slamming door or anything else that might provide a clue as to the source of what I had just experienced.

That feeling! That voice! It was not my imagination. I hurried home, running until I was out of breath. Entering the apartment, I was grateful to hear the familiar, comforting buzz from the air conditioner in my bedroom. It was a relief to feel safe and comfortable after the strange event that had happened just minutes before. Still, I turned on all of the lights, looked in all of the closets, and investigated every possible hiding place, until I was satisfied nothing and no one was there. I staggered into the bedroom and collapsed onto my bed while cursing my foolishness: "You're tired and drunk, your overactive imagination is playing tricks on you." These were the kinds of things I was berating myself with, before falling asleep.

*   *   *

I woke up sweating; I had fallen asleep in my clothes and I could no longer hear the buzzing of my air conditioner. The windows were closed so my apartment had become a sauna. Half-asleep, I staggered to the unit, trying to restart it. And then the weight was there again, and I screamed as the high-pitched voice actually spoke out loud this time, triumphantly declaring "I Clymee!"

That was all I heard – "I Clymee!" – as I spun wildly around – "I Clymee!" – crashing into the bureau in my bedroom – "I Clymee!" – backing hard into the doorframe – "I Clymee!" – falling to the floor and rolling around in every direction – "I Clymee!" – nothing made any difference – "I Clymee!" – the weight on my back became heavier and heavier - "I Clymee!" – I could no longer stand up – "I Clymee!" – now on my stomach, trapped - "I Clymee!" – my ribs crushed from the unseen mass upon me – "I Clymee!" – my spine ... bending – "I Clymee!" – I heard cracking – "I Clymee!" – then I passed out into oblivion.

***

ABOUT THE AUTHOR

About Jeremy Beck's experimental memoir, *Memory Embraced*: "So much writing skill is embedded in this hard-to-categorize but intensely memorable piece that it is the reader's pleasure simply to let go, fully immerse himself and read." – *Readers' Favorite*

Jeremy Beck is a composer whose music has been presented by New York City Opera, American Composers Orchestra, and the Nevsky String Quartet, among others. Recordings of his compositions are available on the innova and Ablaze labels. Jeremy practices law in Louisville, Kentucky.

www.BeckMusic.org

www.ArtsAttorney.net